On *Sesame Street,*
Luis is played by Emilio Delgado.

Library of Congress Cataloging-in-Publication Data
Hautzig, Deborah. Big Bird plays the violin / by Deborah Hautzig ; illustrated by Joe Mathieu. p.   cm. — (A Sesame Street start-to-read book) Summary: Big Bird learns that it takes practice to become a great violin player. ISBN 0-679-81675-5 (trade) : —ISBN 0-679-91675-X (lib. bdg.) : [1. Violin—Fiction. 2. Birds—Fiction. 3. Puppets—Fiction.] I. Mathieu, Joseph, ill. II. Title. III. Series. PZ7.H2888Bj 1991 [E]—dc20 90-8967 CIP AC

Manufactured in the United States of America   10 9 8 7 6 5 4 3 2 1

Big Bird Plays the Violin

by Deborah Hautzig

illustrated by Joe Mathieu

Random House/Children's Television Workshop

One day Big Bird was singing
in his nest.
Betty Lou walked by.
She was carrying a funny-looking case.
"Hi!" said Big Bird.
"What's in that funny-looking case?"

"My violin," said Betty Lou.
"I am taking violin lessons!"
She took out her violin
and played a song for Big Bird.

"Gee, that is beautiful music!"
said Big Bird.
"I wish I had a violin!
Then I could play
beautiful music too!"

"It is not so easy to play
a violin," said Betty Lou.
"You have to practice a lot
and work very hard.
I am going home to practice
right now!"

"WORK?" said Big Bird to himself.
"How can playing a violin be work?"
Big Bird made up his mind.
He was going to find a violin
to play.

Big Bird went to the Fix-it Shop.
"Hi, Luis. I need a violin,"
said Big Bird.
"You do?" asked Luis. "I have never
heard you play the violin."
"That is because I don't have one,"
said Big Bird. "Do you have one
that I can use?"

Luis looked in a closet.
At last he pulled out an old violin.
"This is your lucky day, Big Bird,"
said Luis. "You can borrow this one.
If you really like playing it,
someday you can buy a better one."
"Wow! Thanks, Luis," Big Bird shouted.
"I'll give you a free ticket
to my first concert."

Big Bird ran home.
As soon as he got there
he took out his violin
and began to play.
SCREECH! SCREECH!

Windows opened up and down
Sesame Street.

"What is that awful sound?"
said Bert.
"It sounds like a sick cat,"
said Ernie.

Grover and his mother
looked out their window.
"Oh, my goodness!" said Grover's mother.
"Somebody needs a music teacher!"
She and Grover covered their ears.

Oscar popped up from his trash can.
"Hey, that sounds great!" said Oscar.
"That's my kind of music!"
  Big Bird smiled shyly.
"Thanks," he said.
"I knew I could play
  the violin."

Every day Big Bird played his violin.
He played it at night, too!
It sounded just terrible.
His friends did not know
what to do.

"I do not want to hurt
Big Bird's feelings,"
said Grover with a sigh,
"but his violin playing is
hurting my ears!"

Ernie and Bert
tried to sleep
with earmuffs.

Snuffle-upagus
hid in his cave.

The Count could not bear
to count the notes.

Betty Lou was getting angry.
She tried to practice her violin,
but all she could hear
was Big Bird's screeching violin.

Finally everyone on Sesame Street
got together.
"We have to do something
about Big Bird's violin,"
said Bert.
"I have not slept
for a week!"

"But how can we tell him
how bad he sounds
without hurting his feelings?"
asked Grover.

Suddenly Betty Lou said,
"Hey, everybody! I have an idea.
Follow me!"
They followed her to
Big Bird's nest.

"Hi!" said Big Bird.

"Did you come to hear me play?"

"Not exactly," said Betty Lou.

"We came to help you
    LEARN to play."

"You mean you don't like my music?"
asked Big Bird sadly.

"It isn't music," said Betty Lou.
"Not yet.
But don't feel bad, Big Bird.
Nobody knows how to play the violin
until they LEARN!
That is why I have a violin teacher.
And I will be YOUR teacher."
Big Bird's face lit up.

"Gee, thanks, Betty Lou."

First, Betty Lou showed Big Bird
how to hold his violin.
Then she showed him
how to hold the bow.
"Each string is a different note,"
said Betty Lou.

Big Bird held his violin
and played some notes.
"It does sound better,"
said Big Bird.
"But when will I be able
to play real music?"

"It takes time," said Betty Lou.

"Right!" said Big Bird.

"And practice, practice, practice!
I will practice every day."

"Oh, no!" everyone cried.

Everyone but Oscar.

He said, "Great!"